D0480280

This book belongs to:

_____

_____

_____

First Published 2012 by Brown Watson
The Old Mill, 76 Fleckney Road,
Kibworth Beauchamp, Leic LE8 0HG
ISBN: 978-0-7097-2086-7
© 2012 Brown Watson, England
Reprinted 2013, 2014, 2015

My Little Book of
Stories for
Boys

Brown Watson

ENGLAND

Work and Play

It looks like it is going to be a busy day for Toby the vet. His waiting room is full of people and their poorly pets.

His own cat, Tabitha, wants to play. "Tabitha, you shouldn't be here," says Toby.

Toby sees his first patient. Suri's rabbit has the snuffles. "She needs to take this medicine and stay away from other pets," says Toby. "Bring her back when she is better as her claws need cutting, too."

There are lots of animals to see and Toby has to leave the surgery for some of them. He travels to Farmer Eric's where his sheep dog has hurt his leg.

Tabitha doesn't want to be left out and has sneaked along with him!

Poor Buddy holds up his leg for Toby
to look at. It needs a bandage and
some cream.

"There, that should soon be better," says
Toby. "Good dog. As for you, you naughty
kitten – come on! Time to go home."

Back at the surgery, Toby is checking the X-rays for his next patient. It is hard to concentrate because Tabitha just wants to play!

"Not now, Tabby," says Toby. "I have one more patient to see – and he needs me more than you do right now."

Finally, all of Toby's patients have gone home. He is tidying up when Tabitha jumps up onto the table.

"Okay, okay!" laughs Toby. "I'll look after you now. After all, love and cuddles help to keep all pets happy and healthy!"

In a Muddle

Mr Packard is the postman for Littlehampwick village. Everyone relies on him to deliver their letters, cards and parcels.

Mr Packard loves his job, but sometimes he gets things a bit wrong. He spends too much time daydreaming!

Farmer Eric sees Mr Packard on
his bicycle. "I have a letter for you!"
shouts the postman.
"Erm, that's not my post!" says Farmer
Eric. "This needs to be delivered to the
vet. You've cycled all this way for nothing!"

The vet watches as Mr Packard rummages through his postbag. "There's definitely something in here for you," he says. "I know, because I just tried to deliver it to Farmer Eric!"

The vet laughs and helps Mr Packard sort through the letters.

Mr Packard is daydreaming again
when a loud bark makes him jump. He
drops some of his letters on the floor.

"Ooh, Buster, hello!" he says. "Now look
what I've done! That's lucky – this
letter is for you!"

Mr Packard doesn't always get things wrong. He makes Mrs Hughes very happy when he delivers a parcel from her son in Australia.

She invites him to stop for a cup of tea and some biscuits. Don't forget to take your postbag when you leave, Mr Packard!

Back at the post room, Mr Packard is worried. He has finished his deliveries, but there is some post left.

Surprise! He has been so busy that he forgot it was his birthday. The leftover letters and parcels are cards and presents for him to open!

Emergency!

Being a fire fighter is very exciting. Fireman Joe and Fire Officer Hannah have to be ready to rush off as soon as the alarm sounds.

"Quick – jump in the truck and switch on the siren!"

Fireman Joe is an expert at
driving quickly but safely. The
other drivers must get out of
the way as soon as they hear
the fire engine coming.

Hurry! Mrs Jennings'
washing has caught fire.
Joe needs to guide Mr Jennings
to safety, and then unwind
the hosepipe.

Phew, panic over. Fireman
Joe squirts the flames with
water and the fire goes out.
The washing is ruined,
though!

No time to relax – someone
else needs Fireman Joe's help.
He zooms off to rescue a kitten
that is stuck at the top
of a tree.

Oh, no! Joe wasn't fast enough this time. He arrives at the shop after it has closed. What will he have for his tea? That's a different sort of emergency!

Just the Job

Buddy lives on a farm. He loves it there, but he is feeling sad. A good farm dog should be able to do lots of helpful jobs, but Buddy can't seem to get things right.

Yesterday, Buddy was helping at
the hen house. He held the basket
while Charlie collected the eggs.

But the hens were scared of Buddy.
They flapped and squawked and flew
off in fright. It made Buddy jump
and drop some eggs.

The day before, he was working as a sheep dog. He rounded up all of the sheep and guided them down the hill.

But the sheep ran too far and went straight out of the gate! Buddy had to go round and herd them all up again.

This morning, Buddy tried harder to
do the right thing. He stayed out of
the way while Maddie milked the cows.
She got three full buckets of milk and
was very pleased.

Buddy was pleased too, and jumped
up to lick Maddie's face when she had
finished. She dropped her bucket and milk
poured all over the yard.

"Oh, Buddy!" Maddie sighed, as he licked
up the mess on the floor.
"What shall we do with you?"

Farmer Eric gave Buddy a cuddle to
cheer him up.

"Don't worry, Buddy, I have just the job for
you. I need you to guard the house and play
with the children. I know you will be the best
guard dog and child minder anyone could have!"